CAMPINGLAND

by AME DYCKMAN illustrated by JAMES BURKS

two lions

Text copyright © 2024 by Ame Dyckman
Illustrations copyright © 2024 by James Burks
All rights reserved.

No part of this book may be reproduced, or stored in a retrieval system, or transmitted in any form or by any means, electronic, mechanical, photocopying, recording, or otherwise, without express written permission of the publisher.

Published by Two Lions, New York
www.apub.com

Amazon, the Amazon logo, and Two Lions are trademarks of Amazon.com, Inc., or its affiliates.

ISBN-13: 9781662510830 (hardcover)
ISBN-13: 9781662510823 (digital)

The illustrations were rendered digitally.
Book design by AndWorld Design

Printed in China
First Edition
10 9 8 7 6 5 4 3 2 1

For my family.
I'd do ANYTHING for you, except go camp—
Okay, FINE!
—A. D.

For adventure seekers, big and small, enjoy the journey.
—J. B.

Then we saw a billboard for a **different** kind of camping.

Campingland looked fun and **really** easy!

Not like our first camping trip.

"I'm hot!"

"I'm cold!"

"I'm wet!"

"I'm a little dirty."

There were no bugs in Campingland.

"Welcome!"

BUG FREE

And all the "animals" were well-behaved.

"Want a snack?"

"A chair?"

"Fresh towel?"

Not like our first camping trip.

HEY!

I hugged it.

Our Campingland tent went up fast.

And it **stayed** up.

BEEP!

We couldn't even get lost!

TENT

YOU ARE HERE

Everyone caught a Campingland "fish."

And nobody's Campingland hot dog fell in the dirt.

Or caught fire.

Campingland **did** have fancy bathrooms. With showers, toilets, **and** toilet paper.

Definitely not like our first camping trip.

Our first camping trip was **technically** a disaster, but . . .

Actually, more than a few laughs.

HEE-HEE! That *tickles!*

It wasn't easy or pretty, but our "bad" camping trip still made for **good** family memories. **Real** family memories.

And **that's** how we got kicked out of Campingland.

"FINE!"

"We're going!"

SECURITY

EXIT

It **was** fine. We were ready for a **different** different kind of camping. So...

We packed better.

We're a **little** more experienced.

Whatever happens on **this** trip, we'll just roll with it.

Together!

No matter what.